Tales of
Cats

Also by Pleasant DeSpain

THE BOOKS OF NINE LIVES

VOLUME NINE

Tales of Cats

Pleasant DeSpain

Illustrations by Don Bell

August House Publishers, Inc.

LITTLE ROCK

Published 2003 by August House Publishers, Inc.
P.O. Box 3223, Little Rock, Arkansas 72203
www.augusthouse.com.

Printed in the United States of America

10 9 8 7 6 5 4 3 2 1   HB

LIBRARY OF CONGRESS CATALOGING-IN-PUBLICATION DATA

DeSpain, Pleasant.
      Tales of cats / by Pleasant DeSpain ; illustrations by Don Bell.
          p.   cm. — (The books of nine lives ; v. 9)
      Includes bibliographic references.
      Contents: The king of the cats : England—A kind woman : Israel—
The magnificent cat : Sri Lanka—Hunter cat : Finland—Three children of
fortune : Germany—Why cats live with women : East Africa—The house
of cats : Italy—The boy who drew cats : Japan—The holy cat : Tibet.
      ISBN 0-87483-713-8 (alk. paper)
      1. Cats—Folklore. 2. Tales. [1. Cats—Folklore.   2. Folklore] I. Bell, Don,
1935– ill. II. Title
PZ8.1.D453 Taf 2003
398.24'529752—dc21   2003050209

Executive editor: Liz Parkhurst
Project editor: April McGee
Text designer: Liz Lester
Cover and book illustration: Don Bell

AUGUST HOUSE   PUBLISHERS   LITTLE ROCK

Acknowledgments

I'm fortunate to have genuine friends and colleagues without whose help the continuation of this series would not have been possible. Genuine thanks to:

- Liz and Ted Parkhurst, Publishers
- Don Bell, Illustrator
- April McGee, Project Editor
- Margaret Read MacDonald, Storyteller, Author, Librarian
- Jennifer D. Murphy, Head of the Children's Department, Albany, New York Public Library
- Candace E. Deisley, Youth Services Librarian, Albany, New York Public Library
- Deidre McGrath, Youth Services Librarian, Albany, New York Public Library
- Denver Public Library
- Lakewood, Colorado, Public Library
- Seattle Public Library
- University of Washington Library (Seattle)

The Books of Nine Lives Series

A good story lives each time it's read and told again. The stories in this series have had many lives over the centuries. My retellings have had several lives in the past twenty-plus years, and I'm pleased to witness their new look and feel. Only one of the stories in this volume was originally published in "Pleasant Journeys," my weekly column in *The Seattle Times,* during 1977–78 and later collected into a two-volume set entitled *Pleasant Journeys: Tales to Tell from Around the World,* in 1979. The books were republished as *Twenty-Two Splendid Tales to Tell From Around the World* a few years later and remained in print for twenty-one years and three editions.

Now, in 2003, the time has come for a fresh presentation of these ageless, universal, useful, and so-very-human tales.

I'm profoundly grateful to all the teachers,

parents, storytellers, and children who have found these tales worthy of sharing. One story always leads to the next. May these lead you to laughter, wisdom, and delight. As evolving human beings, we are more alike than we are different, each with a story to tell.

—Pleasant DeSpain
Troy, New York

Contents

Introduction

If you want to be happy in a new home,
a cat must move in with you.
—Russian superstition

Through the eyes of the cat
you may see into another world.
—Irish saying

Cats are animals of power. Worshipped in Egypt, feared as the familiars of witches in Europe, and loved as pets worldwide, cats play the role of trickster with finesse. They can be kind, cruel, independent, or lovable, depending upon the attitudes and beliefs we project onto their changeable characters.

Every cat owner/caregiver I've met has a story to tell about his or her particular cat. There resides in each of those tales a story embodying the essence of "cat." Cats find a way to help reveal our true selves. Thus, a multicultural collection of cat tales is worthy of sharing.

I've included herein tales explaining why cats choose women over men, how cats trick other and (according to cats) lesser animals, how cats overcome obstacles and demons and wait patiently for their time in the sun. I've also included stories showing cats in their glory, magnificence, and generosity.

These tales come from England, Israel, Sri Lanka, Finland, Germany, East Africa, Italy, Japan, and Tibet. Read, enjoy, learn, and tell them again. The cats of the world, as well as your human listeners, will appreciate you.

The King of the Cats

England

Once upon a time, an old woman stirred the pot on the hearth and complained about her husband, who was late in coming home.

"I told Jeremy to come straight from the butchers. I told him not to stop at the ale-house. I told him that I was cooking his favorite stew. Why doesn't he listen?"

Lying on the floor and enjoying the fire's warmth, a large black cat with a white spot on his forehead listened. "Meow, meow," he said.

"You're quite right, Tom Cat," she continued. "I'd be here all alone if it weren't for you. My Jeremy walks to the village to get a chicken for dinner and doesn't come home till the middle of the night. I should make him sleep in the barn. Just see if I don't. And another thing . . ."

She didn't finish her sentence because the cottage door swung open and Jeremy walked in. He carried a plucked bird in one hand and used the other one to hold himself up. He wasn't tipsy from too much ale. He was frightened, frightened nearly to death.

"Jeremy, dear Jeremy, whatever is wrong?" she asked.

"You wouldn't believe it if I told you," he said, sitting in the rocking chair next to the hearth.

"You must tell me. Tom Cat and I have been worried about you all these long hours. Haven't we, Tom?"

"Meow, meow," agreed Tom.

"It was strange, so very strange," began Jeremy. "I bought the hen and stopped by the alehouse for one pint, just one, mind. Then I took the shortcut through the church cemetery. I wish now that I hadn't. I should have taken the long way 'round."

"But you didn't," said his wife, coaxing the story from her husband. "You took the shortcut. Then what happened?"

"I saw a procession of black cats. The moon is half full tonight, and there was just enough light. There were nine of them."

Tom Cat's ears perked up at the mention of nine black cats.

"Nine black cats, you say . . ." said his wife.

"Yes, nine, and they were carrying a small coffin. Four cats were on each side, and the biggest cat was leading them down the pathway. And all nine cats were black and each had a white spot on his head, just

like our Tom."

"Meow?" said Tom Cat, standing up on all four legs and moving closer to Jeremy's chair.

"Would you look at that," said the wife. "Our Tom seems quite interested in your story."

"That he does," agreed Jeremy. "It seems he understands what I'm saying."

"Then what happened?" she asked impatiently.

"They walked right up to me, they did. I stood rooted to the ground with my mouth hanging open. I was shaking all over, like a tree in the wind, but my feet wouldn't run. The lead cat spoke words. I don't know what they mean, but I heard them clear, I did."

Tom Cat stood up on his hind legs placing his forepaws on Jeremy's knee.

"Looks like our cat wants to know what I heard," said Jeremy.

"So do I, so do I," cried his wife.

"It was 'Tell Tom Tildrum that old Tom Toldrum's dead.' That's what he said, just as plain as day, except it was night. But I don't know what it means."

"Who's Tom Tildrum?" asked the wife.

Tom Cat leapt into the air and seemed to

grow to twice his size before landing back on the floor. "I'm Tom Tildrum," he said excitedly. "If Tom Toldrum's dead, then I'm King of the Cats!"

Letting out a screech and yowl, he ran up the chimney and was gone into the night.

The old couple never saw him again.

A Kind Woman

Israel

Long before, when humans and animals were first born, the Lord of the Universe said, "Let each species choose his own place to live and flourish upon the earth."

Humans chose areas that allowed great cities with outlying farmlands. Animals preferred to live in forests, rivers, and deserts. A few of the animals decided to live with humans. Dogs chose to serve hunters, farmers, and rough-and-tumble boys. Cats, having a more particular nature, had a difficult time making up their minds.

With the Lord's blessing, the Cat Kingdom sent a young female to earth to explore the possibilities. Strolling down a city street, the kitty was soon overwhelmed by the sites, sounds, and smells, especially the delicious smells. She stopped at a fish market and sighed, "This is purrrfect. I'll live with the fish seller and help keep the mice away."

The fish seller agreed and locked the small cat in his shop that night, saying, "Kill every mouse you see, and don't eat even one bite of my fish. I'll feed you in the morning."

The cat had a busy night. She pounced on mouse after mouse and got into a horrible fight with a hungry rat. She was tired and hungry by the time morning's first rays of light filled the shop.

The owner opened the door and, seeing all the dead mice on the floor, said, "Well done, little cat. Here's your reward." He tossed her a tiny bite of an old and rotten fish.

The cat ran out the door and down the road, muttering, "He's too cheap to live with. And after all my hard work . . ."

Soon the cat came to a farmhouse. "This looks promising," she said. "There are fields to play in and a big barn with mice to catch. They might even have children who will pet me and make me purr."

The farmer agreed that she could sleep in the barn. "Watch out for the rats, as they grow big out here," he said. "And keep away from the dogs. I have three of them, and they hate cats. And don't let the children tease you too much. They'll pull your tail to make you squeal. Also, the horses tend to kick if you walk behind them. And my cows, now don't let them . . ."

The cat didn't hear what he said about the cows. She was already running down the road as fast as her four cat-feet would carry her. "A farm is not the best place for me," she panted.

Several miles later she came to a small cottage built beside the road. Flowers bloomed in the garden, and the front door stood ajar. Naturally curious, the cat walked in and immediately felt at home. The main room had tall furniture with wooden legs for scratching. In the bedroom she found a soft feather bed and a basket filled with balls of colorful yarn. *Perfect for napping and for playing,* she thought.

A yeasty and delicious odor pulled her toward the kitchen. "It's a loaf of bread in the oven," she said. "How good it smells."

The mistress of the house, a woman of age with kindness written all over her wrinkled face, saw the cat peeking into her kitchen. She smiled and, reaching down to pick her up, said, "My bones are old, little one. I like to sit in my rocking chair while my bread is baking. You sit with me here in my lap."

The cat purred herself to sleep in the com-
forting folds of the old woman's apron. When

she awoke, the mistress gave her a bowl of
sweet milk and a crust of warm bread.

The cat returned to heaven to give her
report.

"Have you decided on the best place for a cat to live?" asked the Almighty Creator.

"Yes," sighed the cat. "In the home of a kind woman who leaves her door ajar."

The Magnificent Cat

Sri Lanka

A kitten was born into the palace of a great ruler. The kitten was soft and cuddly like the finest silk pillow. It was the color of gray mist after a summer rain. The kitten's purr was as loving as a baby's laughter. It was a perfectly exquisite kitten. Everyone agreed that it would grow into the finest cat in the world.

A year later the ruler came to a decision. "I'll offer this magnificent cat to the strongest of the strong. I'll give her to the God of the Sun."

The ruler traveled to the Sun God's kingdom. The Sun was moved by the king's generosity but said, "I'd love to have this perfect cat as my very own. But there is a stronger being in the world who deserves her more. It's the Cloud God. Clouds hide me from view. Take your gift to the strongest."

The earthly king traveled with his cat to the God of the Clouds.

"Yes," said the Cloud God, "she is a superb cat. I've never seen a finer one. I'd love and cherish her, but there is someone stronger. The wind blows me all about the sky. Take her to the Wind God."

The king found the God of the Winds resting in the far northern sky. "Your gift is more than generous," explained the Wind. "I already love this glorious cat. I wish I could accept her, but I'm not worthy. Ants make hills so strong that, no matter how hard I blow on them, I can't knock them down.

Ants deserve her more."

The king carried his precious cat back to earth and met the Ant King.

"She is heaven itself," said the grateful Ruler of Ants. "I'd love to hear her purr each afternoon. There is, however, a stronger being on earth. It's the mighty bull. He tramples my anthills whenever they are in his path. Give your cat to the King of the Bulls."

The ruler now traveled to the bulls' kingdom.

"Indeed I desire this incredible cat for a pet," said the King of the Bulls. "I'd be envied by all others. Yet there is a stronger being among us. Leopard runs me down and kills me for food. Leopard is stronger."

The ruler entered the Leopard King's lair, offering him the cat.

"I'd accept your beautiful gift and be the happiest leopard on earth," said the king, "but I can't. You must give her to my finest teacher, the one who taught me how to climb back down from a tree after first climbing up. Offer her to the King of Cats."

The ruler brought the cat home to his palace. The King of Cats awaited him at the gate.

"She is magnificent," said the Cat King. "I'll make her my wife and love and cherish her always. I thank you for this gift of all gifts."

The wedding was held in the earthly ruler's palace the following week. The Sun God, the Cloud God, the Wind God, the Ant King, the King of Bulls, and the Leopard King were honored guests. The marriage ceremony was nearly as magnificent as the cat herself. The King of Cats and his new wife lived happily together for the rest of their lives.

Hunter Cat

Finland

Wolf and Bear decided to have a feast in celebration of their friendship.

"We are the bravest of the brave," said Wolf. "All the forest animals fear us."

"We are the best hunters as well," said Bear. "We always make a kill."

"Let's make our feast a private affair," said Wolf. "None of the other animals are worthy to eat our food."

"Yes," agreed Bear. "Only the strongest, bravest, and best hunters should attend. That's just you and me."

"You and me!" cried Wolf, and off they ran to make a kill.

Sparrow heard all while sitting on a high branch and decided to have some fun. She flew through the treetops until she spied clever Fox napping near his earthen cave. Singing in his ear, she told him about the private feast.

"And we're not invited?" asked Fox.

"No, just Wolf and Bear."

"That isn't fair," said Fox. "Let's see if we can get them to change their stingy minds."

Fox ran through the thick woods and found Cat playing with a large pinecone. He told Cat about the feast and asked, "How would you like to be a great hunter?"

"Me, a great hunter? I'm just a cat. I hunt mice and the occasional rat, that is, if the rat isn't full-grown. I've never met Wolf and Bear."

"And they haven't met you. That's how I'll be able to turn you into a hunter of wolves and bears," said Fox with a wily grin. "Be brave and do everything I tell you, and I promise you a wonderful feast as reward."

Cat liked the idea of being called a great hunter. "Agreed," he said.

After Fox explained his plan, he and Cat ran to the other side of the forest. They soon spied Wolf and Bear preparing to feast on a plump deer. Just as they began to eat, Fox ran out from behind a tree stump.

"Wait, mighty hunters. I've heard that this feast is for the strongest and bravest of all. There is one more in the forest that deserves to be here."

Bear laughed, saying, "Brother Wolf, is there anyone brave enough to be our brother?"

Wolf laughed, saying, "I think not, Brother Bear."

"You're forgetting Hunter Cat," said Fox. "He's fierce in battle. I watched him attack both a bear and a wolf just last week."

"I've not heard of Hunter Cat," said Wolf.

"Nor have I," said Bear. "Are you sure he hunts bears?"

"Is he big?" asked Wolf.

"Is he smart?" asked Bear.

"You'll soon find out," said Fox. "I told him about your feast. He said he would join you. Listen, I think he's near."

Hiding in the bushes, Cat began to purr, just as he'd been instructed.

"That doesn't sound scary," said Wolf.

"I'm not shaking," said Bear.

"Hunter Cat is just getting warmed up," explained Fox. "It's when he's loud that you must worry."

Cat began to meow. He became louder with each breath.

"I've never heard that before," said Bear. "It makes me a little nervous."

"Yes," said Wolf. "He sounds angry."

Suddenly, Cat screamed in his loudest voice. He screamed and yowled and screamed again. The sound pierced the ears and hearts of Wolf and Bear.

"I'm leaving now," said Wolf. "I'm not scared, but I have to be somewhere else and I'm already late."

"I'm not frightened, either," said Bear. "But I'll join you on your journey if you don't mind, my brother."

Wolf and Bear ran away. Fox called Cat from the bushes and told Sparrow, "Spread the good news. Hunter Cat is holding a feast, and everyone in the forest is invited!"

Cat laughed long and loud. "Thank you, Brother Fox," he said. "It feels good to be a mighty hunter."

Three Children of Fortune

Germany

O nce upon a time, so very long ago, an old father gave each of his three sons a special gift. To the oldest he gave a rooster. To the middle boy he gave a scythe. To his youngest son he gave a cat.

"I'm not long for this world," he said. "And because I'm poor, you must accept these small gifts and make what you can with them."

The oldest son left home and traveled for three months to a distant town in which a rooster had never been seen. The townsfolk didn't even have clocks.

"Friends!" cried the youth. "Look upon my rooster and behold a miracle. Each morning he crows three times to tell me the sun is about to rise. And if he decides to crow in the middle of the day, I know the weather is sure to change."

The people were most impressed and asked if he would sell his marvelous bird.

"Yes," said the boy, "for as much gold as a donkey can carry."

They agreed, and the youth returned home, proud of his treasure.

Now it was time for the middle boy to seek his fortune. He traveled for half a year until he came to a farm community in which the people had never seen or held a scythe. They were puzzled by its curved blade and long handle. They had always pulled the wheat and corn up from the ground, roots and all. The work was hard and slow, and much of the harvest was lost in the process.

The boy began to swing his scythe from one side to the other, across a field of tall wheat. It didn't take long to mow the field clean. The farmers begged the boy to sell his miraculous tool. He agreed, for as much gold as two mules could carry. He soon returned home with his fortune.

The time had come for the youngest lad to venture out into the wide world. He traveled for a year and a day, searching for a town without cats, but had no luck. Cats were everywhere. He booked passage on a ship and, with the cat hidden under his coat, sailed to faraway shores. At last he arrived on a remote island where no one had ever heard of a cat. It was no surprise that the island was overrun with mice.

Even the king had no peace from the multitude of rodents that ran freely throughout the palace. They ate whatever they wanted and squeaked all day long. They took baths in the king's porridge bowl and nibbled at his favorite shoes even while he was wearing them. They climbed up into his bed at night and played hide-and-seek under the sheets!

The youth released his cat in the throne room. Two days and nights went by and

there wasn't a single mouse left in the castle.
The king was so pleased that he rewarded
the boy with a chest of gold and a chest of
diamonds and rubies.

So it was that the third and youngest son
returned home with the largest treasure.
So it was that the three brothers found
their fortunes.

Why Cats Live with Women

East Africa

Long before, in the wilds of East Africa, a young cat decided to find a worthy friend. "My companion must be smart, strong, and most of all, fearless," he said aloud.

The cat watched a beautiful gazelle outrun a pack of hungry hyenas the following afternoon. "She'll make a fine friend," he said.

The cat approached the gazelle that evening. "I admire the way you run," he said. "Let's be friends. We can find food together and keep each other company."

"Yes," said the gazelle. "We can stay alert

and warn each other if danger approaches."

They remained companions for three days and nights. Early on the morning of the fourth day, the cat sensed something wrong. The breeze shifted, and the cat knew that they were in mortal danger. "It's the cheetah," whispered the cat. "Let's set a trap for him."

"No, no, no, no . . ." stuttered the gazelle. "Cheetah frightens me most of all. You run north to distract him. I'll run south. Let's meet at the watering hole this afternoon."

So saying, the gazelle bounded into the air, fleeing to the south. The cat ran north and climbed into the branches of a large tree. He was safe, but disappointed. "Gazelle isn't fearless. I'll have to find a braver companion."

That night he approached the cheetah saying, "My fast friend, you are a warrior. I'd like to be your friend and learn from you."

"Very well," said the cheetah. "I'm often lonely at night, and I'd enjoy your company."

The cheetah and cat made excellent companions for an entire week. Then something unfortunate happened. They were walking through the jungle brush and came upon a baby elephant crying for its mother. "Shhhh," said the cheetah. "The elephant's mother will be enraged if she sees us. She'll blame us for frightening her child."

Suddenly, the mother elephant crashed through the brush, loudly trumpeting her anger.

"Run for your life!" Cheetah yelled.

They escaped the mother elephant, but the cat was again disappointed. "Cheetah isn't fearless after all."

The cat walked over to the watering hole early the next morning to speak with the mother elephant. "You're big and strong," he said with respect. "I like that the other animals fear you so. Could I be a friend to you?"

"Yes," said the elephant. "You can help

keep an eye on my child who likes to wander off even though I tell him to stay close by."

The cat and elephant remained friends for the next two weeks. Whenever danger approached, the mother used her size and strength to keep them safe. The cat continued to be impressed with her until the day a hunter approached the clearing where the elephants slept.

"A man with a spear lurks nearby," the cat whispered into the mother elephant's big ear. "Get ready to frighten him away."

"No," said the elephant. "Men are too dangerous. We will run."

She awakened her child and they ran deep into the jungle, leaving the hunter far behind.

Once again, the cat was disappointed in his choice of companions. "If men scare the elephant, then they must be the bravest of all. I'll be companion to a man."

The cat ran to the village of the humans. He followed the tallest and strongest man to a round hut made of branches and long grass. Just as he was ready to ask the man if he could be his friend, the cat heard the voice of a woman coming from inside the hut.

"Husband, is that you standing outside?"

"Yes, my love, I've just come home. Are you still angry with me?"

"You know I am. I'll be angry for another day or two. Go sleep in your brother's hut. You aren't welcome here."

"Very well, dear wife, whatever you say."

Looking defeated, the man turned and slowly walked away.

Having heard and observed all, the cat knew the truth. "Woman is the strongest of all. She will make the best companion."

This is why, to this very day, cats choose to live with women.

The House of Cats

Italy

Long, long ago, humans and animals could talk with one another. In Tuscany there was a household of wealthy cats who decided to hire a human maid. They spoke with a widow who had two daughters.

"Which of your girls works hardest?" asked the father cat.

"They are both good workers," answered the mother. "Gina is the oldest and is a great help to me. Gabriella, however, is my favorite. She isn't as pretty as her sister, and she doesn't always finish her jobs, but she tries, poor dear, she truly tries."

Gabriella was spoiled. She failed to try hard because she was lazy. Mothers, however, don't like to speak of such things.

Gina was hired to cook, clean, and help take care of all the kittens in the cat household. She was so reliable and did such good work that the cats wanted to give her a special reward. The father cat took Gina into the library. Two beautifully decorated wooden boxes sat on a shelf.

"The box closest to your right hand is filled with dried olives," said the cat. "The one closest to your left hand is filled with gold coins. Choose one as your very own."

Gina thought for a long moment, then answered, "The box of dried olives, please."

The father cat was pleased with her unselfishness. "I insist that you take the box of gold; you've earned it many times over. And you must obey this instruction. Return home to your mother's cottage. When you hear the cock crow, look at him. When you hear the donkey bray, turn your eyes away."

Gina walked home with the box of gold.

As she entered the yard, the cock crowed loudly. The instant she looked at him, a crown made of gold and jewels grew out of her head. The donkey, standing on the other side of the yard, began to bray. Gina quickly turned away.

Both mother and sister were astonished to see Gina with a crown and box of gold coins. She told them all about the cat family and how generous the father cat had been.

"I'll be their maid from now on," said Gabriella. She put on a clean apron and went to town the next day. The cat family agreed to hire her and set her to work. Her duties included cooking, cleaning, and caring for the many kittens. Her meals tasted horrible, and her cleaning was less than thorough. She kicked the kittens when they got in her way. She complained about everything and rested more than she worked. The cat family was unhappy with their new maid.

"Come into the library with me, Gabriella," said the father cat. "I have something to give you."

Two wooden boxes sat on the shelf.

Before the father cat could explain, Gabriella said, "I want the one with the gold coins."

Father Cat grew furious. "You are lazy and wicked. Leave my house at once, and when you hear the donkey bray, don't look at him."

Gabriella stormed home. The moment she entered the yard, the donkey brayed. She looked right at him. The donkey's tail flew through the air and wrapped itself around her head. This was her crown, and it wouldn't come off.

The girls' mother blamed it all on Gina. "You think you are so much finer than your poor sister. You'll do all the work around here from now on. Your sister must stay in her room and rest until that horrible tail is gone from her head."

Gina worked hard each day and never had time to rest. While drawing the bucket from the well one afternoon, a young prince rode into the yard.

"Might I have a drink of that cool water?" he asked.

"Of course, good sir," she said with a curtsey.

The prince couldn't take his eyes away from Gina's beautiful smile. He was just as impressed with the jeweled crown growing from her head. "Do you believe in love at first sight?" he asked.

"I do, indeed," said Gina.

"If I ask you to marry me, will you say yes?"

"Yes, say I. Again I say, yes."

"I'll return tomorrow morning with my carriage and four horses," said the prince. "We'll travel to the castle in style."

Gina's mother, listening from the window, heard all. "If one of my daughters is to be a princess, it will be Gabriella," she said to herself.

She locked Gina in the cellar and told Gabriella to dress in her finest. She pinned a large hat with a thick veil on her favorite daughter's head, covering her face and ugly donkey tail.

When the prince arrived with the coach and horses, he asked, "Why, my dearest, do you hide your beautiful face?"

"A proper husband doesn't see his bride just before the wedding, silly man," she said through the veil.

They rode through the town on the way to the castle. Just as they passed the house of cats, the prince ordered the coachman to stop the horses. "I hear something strange coming from that house," he said. It was the sound of every single cat meowing and calling, calling and meowing, "That's not your proper bride. It's her wicked sister!"

The prince yanked the hat and veil from Gabriella's head. "Where is your sister?" he demanded.

Gabriella told him, and they rode back to the cottage. The prince rescued Gina from the cellar and, after scolding her mother and sister, carried his true love home to the castle. Father Cat and his entire family were honored wedding guests, and the prince and princess lived long and happy lives.

The Boy Who Drew Cats

Japan

In the days of old, a boy was born into a family of poor rice farmers. The baby was small and sickly and didn't grow into a robust youth like his many older brothers and sisters.

"He'll never be able to do his share of work," said his father.

"We must take him to the temple," said his mother. "He'll make a better priest than a farmer."

The boy became an apprentice priest, with lessons to learn and chores to finish. He swept the cold stone floors and helped wash the saffron-colored robes of the priests. He weeded the vegetable garden each day and lit the temple candles each night. He studied hard every afternoon and learned to write using a fine brush and black ink on rice paper.

One day, with just a few strokes of his brush, the boy drew a cat. He showed it to his teacher.

"You have genuine talent," said the old priest. "I want you to practice drawing pictures each day, along with your other lessons."

The boy soon discovered that he loved to draw and paint pictures. He drew temple buildings and the faces of the priests. He drew village children and stray dogs. Most of all, he practiced drawing cats. He drew large cats and small ones, young cats and old ones. He drew cats at play and cats at rest. He drew fighting cats and hunting cats. His cats shimmered with life and seemed ready to leap off the page.

When the boy turned fourteen, the priests made a hard decision.

"You're blessed with a unique talent," they said to the boy. "We feel that you'll become a

better artist than a priest. You must leave this temple and make your own way in the world."

The youth was sad. He had nowhere to go. He couldn't return to his family as a

failed priest. It would bring shame upon
them. He had no one but himself and his talent. Thus he hitched up his robe and began
wearing out his sandals, walking throughout
the countryside. He drew pictures of farms
and families, of animals and buildings, all
along the way. Earning enough from his art
to keep food in his belly, he was able to sur-
vive. Yet he was lonely. He had no place, no
family, and no home.

Late one afternoon, while climbing a steep
mountain path, a fierce rainsquall nearly
washed him off the mountain. He crawled
beneath a rocky ledge, waiting for the storm
to pass, and decided to spend the night. It
wasn't long before an old hermit walked by,
asking if he could share the boy's shelter.

"Yes, grandfather, you may share my rock
and my meal. I have a piece of dried fish and
a rice ball. I'll give you half."

The hermit, impressed with the boy's

generosity, ate the food and heard the boy's story.

"I love to draw," said the youth. "I think the Creator of All Things put me on the earth to draw."

"I believe you, lad. There is an ancient temple at the top of this mountain. Go there. The priests need your talent."

They parted ways the next morning, the hermit heading down the mountain and the boy climbing to the top. He arrived at the temple in the late afternoon. The large stone building was eerily quiet. No chanting came from inside. No birds sang in the nearby trees. He felt unwelcome.

The boy bravely approached the main door and knocked. No one answered.

"Is anyone there? I'll work for food and shelter," he hollered.

No one opened the heavy oaken door.

The lad found a large tree, felled by the

storm the night before, resting against one side of the temple. A branch led to a high window. By climbing the tree, the boy was soon inside the temple's main room. The afternoon light, streaming through the open, narrow windows, swiftly faded into night. The lad used a flint stone to light a candle. The room was large, empty, and carpeted with a thick layer of dust. A white, three-paneled, silk screen stood in one corner. He examined it closely. No marks, decorations, or pictures adorned either side of the panels. The perfect canvas awaited the master's brush.

Using ink he always carried, the youth began to draw. His hand floated across the silk like a feather on a summer breeze. He covered each panel, front and back, from top to bottom and from side to side. Every stroke of his brush became a cat. Large cats and small ones, wild cats and tame ones, cats tumbling in play, cats languid in sleep, cats and even more cats filled the panels to bursting. The cats looked alive. He thought he heard them purr.

"I'm so tired," he said aloud, hiding his cherished brush in the folds of his robe. "I must sleep."

Finding an empty alcove in a nearby room, he snuffed out his candle and fell into a deep sleep. He dreamed a horrible dream. It was a nightmare filled with screaming and fighting and blood. It was the worst night of his young life.

At long last, he awakened to the sound of birds singing for the new day. Rubbing his eyes against the light, he stood up and walked into the main room. He rubbed his eyes again, convinced that the nightmare hadn't ended. His breath stopped and he looked again. What he saw was real.

In the center of the floor lay a huge rat, a demon rat as large as a cow. It was dead. The boy's eyes swung from the rat to the screens. Blood dripped from the jaws and claws of every single cat.

Suddenly the main temple door opened, and a parade of priests walked in. They gazed at the demon on the floor. They looked at the screen. One by one, the priests bowed low before the boy.

"You have saved us from the demon rat," explained the elder priest. "You are welcome here for the rest of your life. Join our family and be our resident artist. You belong here with us. Join our family."

The boy stayed. He drew and painted each day and was honored as one of Japan's greatest artists. He grew old, and when his time came to leave this world, his ashes were buried in the temple courtyard. His favorite brush, used to paint the screens so long before, was buried with him.

The Holy Cat

Tibet

Long ago in the high mountains of Tibet, a clever cat lived in a temple devoted to the wise teacher named Buddha. The priests of the temple, called lamas, wore saffron-colored robes, and each carried a string of prayer beads. The mustard-colored cat found an old string of prayer beads and decided to pretend that he was a devoted lama.

"Let it be known throughout the temple," he said to a family of mice, "that I have reformed my ways. No longer will I be a cruel cat, a killer of mice. Mice need not fear me. Like all good lamas, I'll eat vegetables and rice from now on."

"Is this possible?" asked the mice. "Can a cat become a lama? Are we really safe from you?"

"The Buddha teaches that killing is wrong. I had to change my ways in order to become a holy one. See my prayer beads? I touch one bead for each prayer I say. That's how I keep count."

The mice were impressed and told all the other temple mice about the cat's fresh approach to life. "And," said one of the mice, "the lama-cat offered to teach us the way of the Buddha each morning and afternoon."

Several curious mice sat before the lama-cat the following morning. He sat on a high cushion, just like a real lama, and talked to them about obedience.

"The Buddha says that we must always listen to the lama and do what he says. Be here

on time for the lessons and, when I've fin-
ished, walk in a straight line before me. Do
not look to the right or the left. Do not look

behind you. Look only at me, and I'll give
each of you a blessing."

The lesson was over, and the mice lined
up to parade before the hungry cat. He

touched each on the head, mumbling a quick blessing. Every mouse obeyed, looking neither left nor right nor behind. The last mouse in line reached the cat, and rather than a touch on the head, he received a sharp blow. The other mice filed out of the room, and the cat ate his breakfast.

The mice returned for the afternoon lesson, and again, the last mouse in line provided the cat's dinner. And so it went for several days. The temple mice grew fewer, while the lama-cat grew fatter.

"The cat is behind this," said one of the smartest mice.

"You're right," said his brother. "But how do we discover his secret? No one sees him killing and eating. He acts like a perfect lama."

"I have an idea," said the first brother. "We'll make certain that all the mice who hear the afternoon lesson live another day."

That afternoon, the older brother was first in the blessing line. The younger brother stood last in line. As they moved forward, the older mouse yelled, "I'm still at the front, brother."

"And I'm back here," hollered the younger.

The mice kept moving in a line, each receiving a touch on the head from the cat.

"I'm here, brother," said the older.

"Me too, brother," echoed the younger.

The cat didn't like what was happening. He wouldn't get dinner if they kept it up.

"So far so good, brother," hollered the older.

"I'm alive back here," said the younger.

The cat was angry as well as hungry. The blessings continued. The mice continued to obey the teachings of the master, looking neither left nor right nor behind.

"I'm still here at the front, brother," said the older.

"I'm still back here," said the younger.

The cat couldn't help himself. Dropping the prayer beads, he leapt from the cushion in a rage.

"Run for your lives!" yelled both brother mice, scurrying to safety.

The cat bounded about the temple room, desperately trying to catch his meal. All the mice made it to safety. The yellow cat threw away his prayer beads and soon left the temple. The brother mice had bested him.

Buddha says: *Tricks on others lead to defeat.*

Notes

The stories in this collection are my retellings of tales from throughout the world. They have come to me from written and oral sources and result from thirty years of my telling them aloud.

One of these tales (indicated by an asterisk) was previously included in my two-volume set entitled *Pleasant Journeys: Tales to Tell From Around the World* (Mercer Island, Washington: The Writing Works, 1979) and later renamed *Twenty-Two Splendid Tales to Tell From Around the World* (Little Rock: August House, 1990).

Motifs given are from *The Storyteller's Sourcebook: A Subject, Title and Motif Index to Folklore Collections for Children* by Margaret Read MacDonald (Detroit: Neal–Schuman/Gale, 1982); and *The Storyteller's Sourcebook: A Subject, Title and Motif Index to Folklore Collections for Children 1983–1999* by Margaret Read MacDonald and Brian W. Strum (Detroit: Gale Group, 2001).

The King of the Cats—England

Motif B342.1. *Cats are shifty creatures* is part of cat lore throughout the world. My first encounter with this story resulted from a high school English assignment in which I read tales collected by Joseph Jacobs.

Variants abound. See *More English Fairy Tales*

by Joseph Jacobs (London: David Nutt, 1894), pp. 156–158; and *Fairy Tales From the British Isles* by Amabel Williams-Ellis (New York: Warne, 1960), pp. 106–109. A Dutch version is found in *Cat Tales* by Natalia M. Belting (New York: Holt, Rinehart & Winston, 1959), pp. 21–27.

A Kind Woman — Israel

Motif A2500. I first encountered an anecdote in a five-line, written source, leading to this tale. See *Folktales of Israel* by Dov Noy (Chicago: University of Chicago Press, 1963), p. 64. Building up the story during several years of telling it aloud, I tend to slightly exaggerate the four characters (cat, fish seller, farmer, and woman of age) to express how new everything is for young cat.

Another variant is found in *Cat Lore* by Marjorie Zaum (New York: Atheneum, 1985), pp. 37–42.

The Magnificent Cat — Sri Lanka

Motif L392.0.4. A variant of the Chinese tale, "The Extraordinary Cat" (see *The Books of Nine Lives, Volume Two: Tales of Nonsense and Tomfoolery* by Pleasant DeSpain [Little Rock: August House, 2001], pp. 39–42), this tale is worth telling again. I heard this version at a dinner party in Colombo, Sri Lanka, in 1999.

Another variant is found in *The Toad is The Emperor's Uncle: Animal Folktales From Vietnam* by

Vo-Dinh (Garden City, New York: Doubleday, 1970), pp. 123–128.

Hunter Cat—Finland

Motif K2324. This is my retelling of a story initially encountered in *Tales From a Finnish Tupa* by James Cloyd Bowman and Margery Bianco (Chicago: Albert Whitman, 1936), pp. 245–246.

For the Russian variant see *Tales From Atop a Russian Stove* by Janet Higonnet-Schnopper (Chicago: Albert Whitman, 1973), pp. 82–90. A Polish version is found in *The Jolly Tailor and Other Fairy Tales* by Lucia Merecka Borski & Kate B. Miller (New York: McKay, 1928, 1956), pp. 245–246.

Three Children of Fortune*—Germany

Motif N411.1.B. Perhaps the best known variant of this age-old "Dick Whittington" tale is "Puss and Boots," which I heard as a child.

The French version is found in *Animal Stories* by Walter De La Mare (New York: Scribner's, 1940), pp. 128–132. The German variant is found in *Grimms' Fairy Tales* by Jakob Ludwig Karl Grimm and Wilhelm Grimm (New York: Grosset and Dunlap, 1945), pp. 23–26. A delightful Italian variant is found in *The Priceless Cats and Other Italian Folk Stories* by M.A. Jagendorf (New York: Vanguard, 1956), pp. 47–58.

Why Cats Live with Women—East Africa

Motif A2513.2.1. This tale was told by one of my high school students during a summer course at the College of the Virgin Islands, St. Thomas, in 1967. After much searching, I was delighted to find a written variant in *When the Stones Were Soft: East African Fireside Tales* by Eleanor B. Heady (New York: Funk & Wagnalls, 1968), pp. 85–89.

The House of Cats—Italy

Motif Q2.1.1Ca. A Tuscan tale in classic fairy tale form, this "Cinderella" story works well with children under the age of seven. I first encountered it in *The Crimson Fairy Book* by Andrew Lang (New York: Longmans, Green, 1903), pp. 219–228. See also *The House of Cats and Other Stories* by John Hampden (New York: Farrar, Straus & Giroux, 1966), pp. 3–8.

The Boy Who Drew Cats—Japan

Motif D435.2.1.1. Taken with his prosaic stories, I became a fan of the Japanese aficionado Lafcadio Hearn in the late 1960s. This ancient Japanese folktale made a lasting impression. I've told it hundreds of times to thousands of listeners.

See *The Boy Who Drew Cats and Other Tales* by Lafcadio Hearn (New York: Macmillan, 1963), pp. 14–20. Another variant is found in *Wonder Tales of*

Dogs and Cats by Francis Carpenter (New York: Doubleday, 1955), pp. 195–203.

The Holy Cat — Tibet

Motif K815.16.1. Having meditated in several Buddhist temples throughout Southeast Asia and in the West, I find sharing this Tibetan tale great fun. I first encountered it in *Animal Folk Tales* by Barbara Ker Wilson (New York: Grosset & Dunlap, 1971), pp. 123–125.

A Chinese variant is found in *Tricky Peik and Other Picture Tales* by Jeanne B. Hardendorff (Philadelphia: Lippincott, 1967), pp. 27–32.